If I Were a Tree

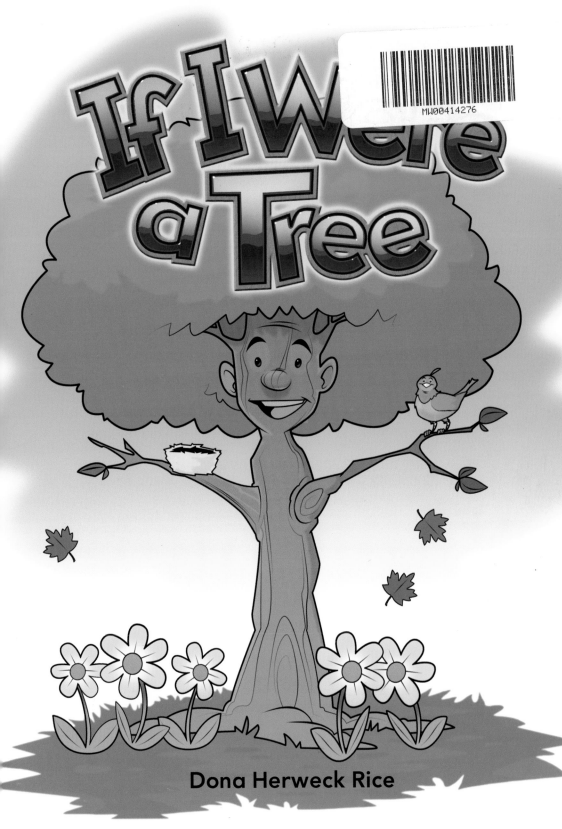

Dona Herweck Rice

If I were a tree,
I'd grow straight and high.

And touch my branches
way up to the sky.

4.

I would dig my roots
down far and down deep.

I'd grow in the spring.

In winter I'd sleep.

The birds in their nests would all live on me.

16